DISNEY · PIXAR

WALL·E

~ BOOK EIGHT ~

DISNEY PRESS
New York · Los Angeles

WALL • E was a Waste Allocation Load Lifter, Earth class. His job was to compact the trash humans had left behind when they abandoned Earth. WALL • E was lonely. He wanted someone to love. One day, WALL • E was out compacting and cubing trash when he found something special. It was a plant.

That night, another robot landed on Earth. WALL•E fell
in love with the sleek new robot at first sight. Her name was
EVE. WALL•E realized that EVE was looking for something
on Earth. But she wouldn't tell him what it was.

WALL•E took EVE to his home and showed her all the
treasures he had collected from the trash.

WALL•E reached for EVE's hand, then lost his nerve and turned away. Remembering the plant, he took it out and showed it to her. EVE snatched up the plant. She stored it inside her chest and shut down.

WALL•E shook her. "Ee-vah? Ee-vah?" he cried. But it was no use. EVE would not wake up.

The next day, as WALL•E left for work, the ground shook. EVE's spaceship had returned.

A robot arm lifted EVE into the ship's cargo hold.

WALL•E did not want to lose EVE. He climbed onto the ship and held on tight.

The spaceship docked inside an enormous ship called the *Axiom*. When EVE emerged, a cleaner robot named M-O scanned her.

"Foreign contaminant," M-O said. He shuddered and started scrubbing.

Just then, a robot named Go-4 approached. He moved EVE into a transporter and began to drive.

WALL•E followed EVE to the bridge. A robot pilot named Auto was guiding the ship.

"Captain, you are needed on the bridge," Auto called.

The captain rose to the bridge in a hover chair.

"Captain, Probe One has returned positive," Auto said.

EVE's plant had set off the ship's sensors. It was time to return to Earth!

But when EVE opened her chest, the plant was gone!

"The probe must be defective," the captain said. "Send her to the repair ward."

In the repair ward, WALL•E thought the robots were hurting EVE. He tried to rescue her, but the other robots ended up chasing them.

EVE led WALL•E to an escape pod and helped him inside. When he saw that she wasn't coming with him, he jumped back out.

Suddenly, the robots heard something approach the escape pod. It was Go-4. He had the missing plant!

Setting it in the pod, Go-4 went to the controls. When he turned around, WALL•E was proudly holding the plant.

Go-4 hit a button, shooting the pod—and WALL•E—into space. As soon as Go-4 left, EVE leaped out of the shadows. She opened an air lock and rocketed off after WALL•E.

In the pod, WALL•E heard the computer say, "Ten seconds till self-destruct." Go-4 had set the pod to explode!

Outside, EVE watched in horror as the pod blew up. Just then, a fire extinguisher sputtered by. Hanging on to it was WALL•E! He had saved the plant and escaped the pod!

EVE locked the plant inside her chest, then leaned her head against WALL•E's. A spark passed between them.

WALL•E and EVE snuck back into the ship, only to find the entrance to the bridge blocked. Suddenly, EVE had an idea.

EVE climbed through the trash chute, bursting out in the captain's quarters. She opened her chest to reveal the plant.

The captain was stunned. "How . . . how'd you find it? We can go back home!" he cried.

Pressing a button, the captain viewed EVE's memories of Earth. All he saw was trash. He slumped in defeat. There was nothing to go home to.

EVE was watching, too. She saw different memories: WALL•E rescuing the plant, protecting her from the rain, keeping watch over her day and night.

Meanwhile, inside the trash chute, WALL•E waited for EVE.

The captain stared at the plant. Trash or no trash, he was ready to go home. But Auto refused to turn the ship.

The robot pushed a button and a man appeared on the captain's screen. "Operation: Cleanup has failed," the man said. "Go to full autopilot. Do not return to Earth!"

The captain stared at the date. The message had been recorded seven hundred years ago!

Auto beeped an order, and Go-4 appeared. He snatched the plant from the captain and threw it down the garbage chute.

As if by magic, the plant reappeared. WALL•E had caught it!

Auto attacked WALL•E, throwing him back down the chute. Then he shut down EVE and dumped her into the chute, too.

EVE rebooted. She and WALL•E were on a garbage heap. M-O was there, too. WALL•E had been badly hurt in the fall.

"Earth," he said.

EVE understood. The parts to fix WALL•E were back on Earth, in his truck.

EVE scooped up WALL•E and M-O, blasted a hole in the ceiling, and took off.

Meanwhile, on the bridge, the captain jumped Auto. With a lunge, he slammed a button on the console. On the deck below, a holo-detector popped up, ready to accept the plant and begin the trip home.

Auto threw the captain to the floor. "Desist!" he cried.

Auto spun his wheel and the ship tilted dangerously to one side.

The ship's passengers fell out of their hover chairs and slid into a giant pile. In the confusion, WALL•E dropped the plant. It was buried beneath the passengers.

Auto switched off the holo-detector. It began to retract, but WALL•E wedged himself under it. Auto was enraged. He reversed the holo-detector, damaging WALL•E and snapping off his joints.

Suddenly, the captain stood up! He reached for the control panel and flipped the "auto" button to "manual."

"You are relieved of duty," he told Auto with a smile.

On the deck below, M-O found the plant. EVE shoved it into the holo-detector. The computer recognized the plant and set a course for Earth.

When the ship touched down on Earth, EVE hurried to WALL•E's truck. She quickly installed a new circuit board in the robot. WALL•E's eyes opened, but there was no life in them. He moved about mechanically, collecting trash. He wasn't WALL•E anymore.